NOODLE

ELLEN MILES

SCHOLASTIC INC.
New York Toronto London Auckland Sydney
Mexico City New Delhi Hong Kong Buenos Aires

If you purchased this book without a cover, you should be aware that this book is stolen property. It was reported as "unsold and destroyed" to the publisher, and neither the author nor the publisher has received any payment for this "stripped book."

No part of this publication may be reproduced, stored in a retrieval system, or transmitted in any form or by any means, electronic, mechanical, photocopying, recording, or otherwise, without written permission of the publisher. For information regarding permisson, write to Scholastic Inc., Attention: Permissions Department, 557 Broadway, New York, NY 10012.

ISBN-13: 978-0-545-03457-9
ISBN-10: 0-545-03457-4

Copyright © 2008 by Ellen Miles. All rights reserved. Published by Scholastic Inc. SCHOLASTIC, LITTLE APPLE, and associated logos are trademarks and/or registered trademarks of Scholastic Inc.

Cover art by Tim O'Brien
Designed by Steve Scott

12 11 10 9 8 7 6 5 4 3 2 8 9 10 11 12 13/0

Printed in the U.S.A.

First printing, May 2008

For Mary and Leverett

CHAPTER ONE

"Brrr!" Lizzie folded her arms across her chest and tucked her chin into her jacket collar. "I'm *freezing*! Whose idea *was* this, anyway?" She glared at her father. She knew exactly whose idea it was. Who else in the Peterson family would think that it was a good idea to have a Saturday afternoon picnic at Loon Lake Park — in *March*?

On summer days, Loon Lake Park was one of Lizzie's favorite places. The lake was just the perfect size, not too small and not too big. On a Saturday afternoon in July, the water would be a sparkling sweep of crystal blue instead of a flat plain of rough gray ice. The sun would be blazing, but there would be cool, shady places under the towering trees near shore. The green, grassy slope where people parked their beach chairs and coolers in summer was now just a dingy patchwork of leftover snow and mud. In summer, the park's sandy beach, playground, and campground would be alive with activity: Kids and moms and dads would be swimming and fishing and paddling canoes, climbing the jungle gym and playing catch, and buying Popsicles from the little store. There would be that special, only-in-summer smell in the air, a mix of hot dogs grilling and suntan lotion and newly-mowed grass. Now it was totally quiet and empty except for the Petersons.

Lizzie looked across the frozen lake. There were a few little houses — cabins, really — along the far shore. Each one had its own little beach, a dock, and maybe a canoe or a rowboat. Nobody was at the cabins now, but in summertime they'd be full of people, just like the park was.

Lizzie sometimes pretended that the smallest cabin, the one with moose antlers over the

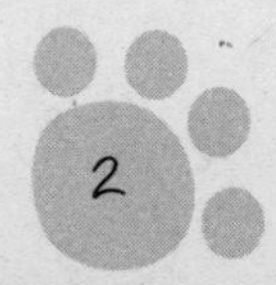

doorway, was hers. She liked to imagine waking up early and starting her day by doing a cannonball off its dock, right into the still, blue water. The gates at the park entrance didn't even open until ten A.M., but if you had your own cabin you could swim whenever you wanted.

Dad said those cabins cost a ton of money. Since he was a firefighter and Mom was a newspaper reporter, the Petersons were not exactly millionaires. That meant they could not afford a cabin at Loon Lake.

At least they lived nearby, so they could visit as often as they liked. They came all the time in the summer — and they always came at least once in the winter, too. Dad said their winter picnic was "a highlight" of his year. He said he and Mom used to go on winter picnics all the time. They would bring binoculars to look for winter birds, plenty of food, and blankets to keep them warm. That was long ago, before Lizzie and her two younger brothers, Charles and the Bean (his real name was Adam, not that anybody ever called him that), were even born.

It wasn't that Lizzie really minded the winter picnics. It was fun to help load up the basket with blankets and thermoses full of hot cocoa and spicy chili. She liked the part where she and Dad made a fire in one of the picnic area fireplaces. And she could even deal with sitting on the cold, hard ground, poking a marshmallow on a stick into the dying coals. What she *didn't* like was how it always took Mom and Dad so long to choose the exact right spot for the picnic.

"How about over by the marsh?" Mom asked now. "We might see some interesting birds or some animal tracks."

"I like that spot by the boat docks," Dad answered. "It has the best view of the lake."

Lizzie and her brothers stood there, shivering and looking out at the grayish-white frozen lake and the bare, brown trees along its shore. A stiff

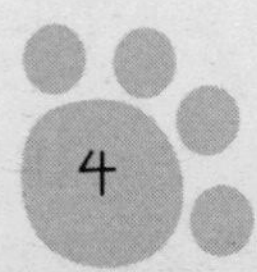

breeze stung Lizzie's cheeks. "Come *on*, you guys! I'm *freezing*!" she repeated.

"*I* warm!" the Bean proclaimed. He pointed to his chest. "I *very* warm in my Fur."

Lizzie rolled her eyes. The thing about the Bean was that he liked to pretend he was a puppy. He liked to take naps on a doggy bed, eat doggy snacks, and play with doggy toys. Lizzie had always thought all that stuff was kind of cute.

But lately, the Bean was doing something that was not quite so cute. He had been wearing his "Fur" — a brown, fuzzy fleece sweater that Mom had found on sale — all day long, every single day. He even slept in it! The only time he took it off was when he took a bath, and then he insisted that it had to be hanging on a hook in the bathroom where he could see it.

Mom had tried to take the Fur away to wash it, but the Bean got pretty upset about that. Mom believed in "picking her battles" with a toddler, and she didn't think the Fur was worth arguing

about. She had promised to let the Bean be the one to decide when and if to wash his Fur — even if it took forever.

That was fine for Mom, but Lizzie was really getting sick of seeing the Bean in his Fur. By now it was kind of smelly and crusty, with blotches of grape juice and bits of mud and oatmeal stuck to it.

But there was nothing Lizzie could do about it. The Bean was not about to give up his Fur. Anyway, that wasn't the point right now. The point was, Lizzie was freezing. And so was the Petersons' *real* puppy. "Look at poor Buddy. He's shaking!"

All the Petersons looked down at their puppy, Buddy. He looked back up at them with his big, chocolate-brown eyes. Then he held up one little tan paw.

My feet are cold! Why are we just standing around? Maybe we'd warm up if we ran around or had something to eat.

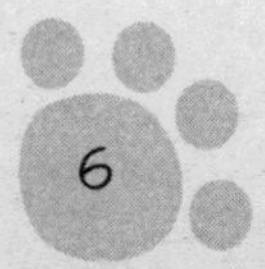

"Aww!" said Dad. "He *is* cold, the poor little guy."

"Don't worry, Buddy," Mom said. "We'll get a fire going right away." She bent down to give him a kiss and stroke the little white heart-shaped area on his chest. Then she straightened up and looked at Dad. "The place by the docks sounds fine," she said.

Charles grinned at Lizzie and gave her a thumbs-up. "Good thinking," he whispered. Like her, he knew that everybody in the family could always agree about one thing: Taking good care of Buddy was very important.

They all loved Buddy so much. He was the smartest, cutest, sweetest puppy *ever*. The Petersons had met lots and lots of puppies. As a foster family, their job was to take care of puppies who needed homes. They gave the puppies a safe place to live while they looked for the perfect forever family for each one. But when they met Buddy, they knew exactly where his perfect home was: It was right there with them. Now he was part of their family.

One of the best things about the winter picnic was that Buddy could come. Dogs weren't allowed at Loon Lake Park in the summertime. Lizzie understood that the crowded, hot beach was not a great place for dogs — but still, she always hated leaving Buddy home alone while the rest of the family was having fun. On summer days she had sometimes seen a black dog diving off a long dock by her favorite little cabin across the lake. Buddy would have *loved* to do that!

Lizzie knew she was lucky to be able to go to Loon Lake Park. But sometimes she could not help envying the people — and dogs! — who had their own places on the lake.

"Can I let Buddy off the leash to run around?" Lizzie asked her dad now.

Dad looked out at the lake. "Better not," he

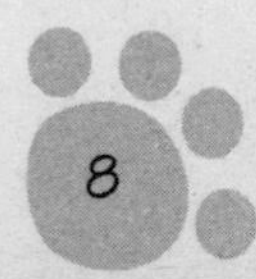

said. "That ice looks a little thin. It's been warmer the last few days, and the ice is starting to melt in places. We wouldn't want Buddy to fall in. The water would be very cold and dangerous for a dog."

Lizzie knew her dad was probably right. "Sorry, Buddy," she said. She was sure he would have loved to run along the lakeshore, his ears flapping in the chilly breeze. "How about if you help me find some sticks?"

Sticks? I love sticks! Let's go!

Buddy tugged at his leash, pulling Lizzie toward a patch of woods near a little curve in the lakeshore. "Look! He can't wait to help!" Lizzie said. She trotted after the strong little puppy, laughing whenever he picked up a stick and carried it proudly, his tail waving like a flag.

Buddy only took a few steps with each stick

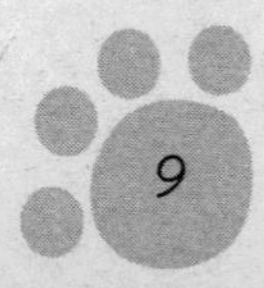

before he got bored and dropped it so he could look for a new one. Lizzie followed behind, stooping to pick up each one he dropped. Soon she had an armload, almost enough for a fire.

Buddy was still pulling her along the lakeshore. But now Lizzie noticed that his head was raised, his nose was twitching, and his ears were all perked up. Lizzie knew that meant her puppy had seen or heard something interesting.

"What is it, Buddy?" Lizzie asked. She followed his gaze, out toward the lake. Lizzie saw a dark circle, way out in the middle of the flat, grayish ice. Open water! And — was there something *swimming* in it?

Lizzie dropped her armload of sticks. "Come on!" She pulled on Buddy's leash. "Come on, Buddy!" She ran as fast as she could, back toward her family. Charles and the Bean were down by the lakeshore. Mom and Dad were still unpacking all the picnic stuff.

"Mom — Dad — quick — I need binoculars — something —" Lizzie was out of breath by the time she reached them.

"What's up, Miss Lizzie?" Dad asked.

"Binoculars, binoculars," Mom murmured, poking through one of the bags. "Here they are! Did you see an interesting bird?"

"Maybe." Mom handed Lizzie the binoculars. By now she had caught her breath. "I don't know. It might be a bird, or an otter, or some other kind of animal. But whatever it is, I think it's stuck out there in a circle of open water!"

She pointed, and Mom and Dad peered out onto the lake. "That dark spot?" Dad asked. "Is that the open place?"

"Mmm-hmm." Now Lizzie was looking through the binoculars. Everything was all blurry at first, until she turned the focus knob. She couldn't find the dark spot on the lake, but then, suddenly, she could see everything.

"Oh, no!" Lizzie felt her body go hot all over, then cold again.

"What is it?" Mom asked. "Lizzie? Honey?"

Lizzie could hardly get the words out. "It's . . . it's a puppy!"

CHAPTER TWO

"A puppy!" Mom took the binoculars and held them to her eyes. "Oh, my! I think you're right!" She handed the binoculars to Dad. "Poor thing! He must have run out onto the frozen lake. Think how surprised he must have been when the ice broke underneath him!"

Dad took one look, gave the binoculars back to Mom, and pulled his cell phone out of his jacket pocket. "Uh-oh," he said, looking at the screen. "Hardly any battery power left. I have *got* to find my charger." He punched in some numbers. "Oh, good. It's dialing. Hello, Bill?" he said. "Paul Peterson here. We need the cold-water rescue team *now*, down at Loon Lake Park." He listened for a moment. "No, it's not a person,"

he said. "It's a dog. A puppy, in big trouble." After another second, he snapped his cell phone shut. "They'll be here as soon as they can," he told Lizzie and Mom.

Charles came running over with the Bean trotting after him. "What's going on?"

"There's a puppy out there." Lizzie pointed toward the lake. "See that dark place? That's open water. And there's a little puppy swimming around and around in it. I saw him trying to claw his way out, but the ice on the edge of the circle just breaks. He can't get out! He could drown!"

"But he won't," Mom said quickly. "Dad called down to the fire station and alerted the cold-water rescue team. They'll be here any second."

"Uppy?" asked the Bean, looking worried. He didn't quite get what was going on, but he understood that there was a puppy involved and that people were upset.

"Yes, a puppy," Lizzie said. She bent down to

hug the Bean. Buddy jumped up to lick the Bean's cheek. "But the puppy will be okay." To herself, Lizzie added, *I hope.*

The Bean was distracted by Buddy's licking. He laughed his googly laugh and squeezed Buddy tight with both arms. Buddy gave a little *whuff*.

Charles wasn't so easily distracted. "But *how* will they save him?" he asked. Mom had helped him focus the binoculars and now he was peering through them, across the frozen lake. "He's so little! And I think he's really scared! His mouth is open wide, like he's panting for breath."

Lizzie took the binoculars and looked again. The puppy seemed to be swimming more slowly now. Lizzie felt her stomach twist into a knot. The poor little guy! He must be terrified.

"Here they are!" Dad was waving his arms at a boxy red emergency truck that was bouncing down the muddy slope, picking its way between patches of snow. "This way! Over here!"

The truck stopped and four people piled out. Two of them were dressed from head to toe in thick red rubber suits with red rubber hoods. "Peterson!" one of them said. "What's up?"

Dad pointed out toward the lake. "Out there," he said. "We think it's a puppy."

The rescuers grabbed bundles of rope and other equipment from the back of their truck and ran for the shoreline.

"Dad." Lizzie tugged at her father's sleeve. "How are they going to save the puppy?"

"See Tyler and Emily, in the red suits?" Dad asked. "They probably pulled those outfits on while they were on their way here. They're a special kind of wet suit, made for really cold water. If the rescuers fall in, the suits will protect them."

As he talked, he and Lizzie and the rest of the family were trotting down to the shore, to be closer to the action.

"I don't know if you noticed," Dad went on, "but

there are hooks on each suit where they can attach a rope. See? They're clipping in now."

"So the other guys can use the rope to haul them out if the ice breaks and they fall in?" Charles asked.

"Exactly. This team practices all the time. They know what they're doing," Dad said. "But it's still dangerous."

Lizzie held her breath as Tyler, one of the red-suited rescuers, began to crawl out onto the ice. He was practically on his belly, like a snake. Would the ice break right away?

"And there goes the other one," said Mom.

Sure enough, Emily had begun to crawl behind Tyler. So far, the ice was still holding them both. Their ropes trailed behind them, held by the men on shore.

Dad was watching through the binoculars. "That puppy sure does look tired," he said. "I hope they get to him soon."

"Can I see?" Lizzie took the binoculars and

peered through them. What she saw made her heart flip over. The little dog was barely keeping his head above water. But, as she watched, she saw his ears perk up and his eyes brighten. She moved the binoculars to see what he was looking at. The two figures — bright red against the gray ice — were crawling closer to the open water. "I think the puppy sees them coming!" she said.

Lizzie handed the binoculars back to her dad. She squinched her eyes shut, crossed her fingers, and wished *hard* that the rescuers would get there in time.

Crack! Lizzie's eyes popped open and her hand flew to her mouth. "Oh, no!" she said as she watched a long black line drawing itself across the gray surface of the lake. Then she saw another line, and another. *Crack! Crack! Crack!* Tyler and Emily were only a few feet away from the open water where the puppy was trapped — and now the ice was breaking, right underneath them!

Then, without another sound, the ice near the two rescuers seemed to disappear, leaving nothing but dark, cold water around the two red suits. And as Lizzie watched, the water swallowed those red suits right up.

CHAPTER THREE

The two red-hooded figures bobbed back up a second later. They hooted and waved at the men on shore to show that they were all right.

"Too risky! We're gonna haul you in!" yelled one of the men on shore. "Ready?" He started to pull on the rope.

But Emily was facing the other way — toward the puppy. "Hold on!" she shouted. "I think I can get him!" Sure enough, the ice had broken all the way over to the circle of open water. The puppy was only a few yards away from Emily. She started to splash her way toward the puppy, swimming awkwardly in her big red suit.

Lizzie held her breath. She could hardly even

stand to watch. "Is Emily going to make it?" She looked up at her dad, who was frowning as he peered through the binoculars. Then, suddenly, he smiled.

"Yeah!" he yelled, pumping his fist. He was still looking through the binoculars. "Got him!"

Lizzie looked back out at the lake. Sure enough, Emily was splashing back in their direction — with the puppy tucked under one red rubber arm. Lizzie felt tears prickling her eyes.

Dad handed her the binoculars. "Stay here for a second so you're out of the way. I'm going to go help pull Emily in," he said. He dashed down to the shore and grabbed the rescuer's rope, falling into place behind the other men. They all leaned back with their feet planted on the ground, like they were playing tug-of-war.

Lizzie peered through the binoculars. Now she could see the puppy clearly. He looked wet and cold and miserable — but surprisingly, not too scared! He wasn't struggling at all. Emily had stopped trying to swim and was just holding the puppy tight as the guys on shore reeled her in like a giant red fish. Now that she could see him better, Lizzie thought the puppy looked about four months old. He was a little smaller than Buddy.

Soon Tyler was on shore, and then the whole team was hauling on the rope, pulling Emily in. It wasn't long before the rescuer and her precious cargo were standing on shore, dripping wet.

Mom had been rummaging in the baskets. "Let's go warm that puppy up!" she said. "Lizzie, Charles, take these blankets. The Bean and I will go start our van and get the heater going." She tossed an armload of blankets to Lizzie. Lizzie and Charles took them and ran as fast as they could toward the puppy.

Down at the shoreline, Tyler and Emily looked exhausted — but happy. The guys who had hauled them in were slapping them on the back, congratulating them. When Emily saw Lizzie and the

blankets, she strode right over. “Good idea!” she said. “This little guy sure does have the shivers.”

Emily handed the puppy to Lizzie. For the first time, she got a good look at him. Even though he was soaking wet, he was adorable. His long, curly fur was frozen into dark spiky points at the moment, but Lizzie thought she'd see soft golden curls when it was dry. He also had long, floppy ears, the cutest little black nose, and a soft, pink, puppy belly.

Lizzie looked down into the puppy's dark brown eyes and something happened.

Lizzie fell in love.

Oh, sure, Lizzie fell in love with *every* puppy she met. But this was different. There was something about this puppy that made Lizzie's heart just melt. What was it?

There was no time to wonder about that now. This little pup was shivering all over. He needed to warm up fast.

Quickly, Lizzie wrapped the puppy in a

blanket, and then another one, so that only his darling nose showed. She held him tight against her chest.

"That was awesome!" Charles was saying to Tyler. "I want to join your team someday."

"We can always use new members!" Tyler stopped coiling rope for a moment to talk to Charles. "You're welcome to come watch one of our training sessions. Your dad can tell you when and where."

Dad shook hands with all the rescuers. "Great job," he said.

"What about the puppy?" asked Emily. "What will you do with him now?"

Lizzie looked at her dad. "He's not wearing a collar, and I don't see anybody searching for him. He must be lost."

"I didn't notice any tracks out there on the ice," said Tyler. "That part of the lake is probably still frozen too hard for footprints. Hard to say *where* he came from."

Lizzie hugged the bundled puppy even closer. The poor little thing. He must be so scared and lonely. “Can we take him?” she asked. “Just until we find out where he belongs?” Her heart was thumping. What if Dad said no?

But Dad nodded. “Of course. I’m sure Mom will agree. We’d better stop to see the vet on the way home and get him checked out. He seems fine, but I’d like to make sure.”

Lizzie and Charles grinned at each other. All right! A new foster puppy! How exciting. This was turning out to be the best winter picnic ever, even though they were leaving before the picnic part even happened.

Mom was waiting for them in the nice warm van. She had packed all their stuff, and the Bean was already buckled into his car seat. Buddy was in the way back, safe inside his travel crate. “We’re all ready to go,” Mom said. “Here’s what I think: I think we should take this puppy home, just until we find out where he belongs. But we’d better stop at the vet's first, just to make sure he's all right."

Lizzie, Dad, and Charles started to laugh. "That is *exactly* what we were just saying," Dad said. "Great minds think alike!"

"Great minds?" Charles looked bewildered.

"It's just an expression," Lizzie told him. "Here, hold the puppy while I get in." She handed over her bundle, then climbed into the van. As soon as she had her seat belt buckled, she held out her arms and Charles reluctantly gave the puppy back. Lizzie snuggled her chin down into the blankets and gave the puppy's nose a kiss. "You're safe now," she told him. The puppy had already stopped shivering. He looked back at Lizzie with big, shiny eyes. She felt her heart melt again.

"I wonder what breed this puppy is," she said. "With this curly fur, he looks kind of like that poodle named Fiona who goes to Aunt Amanda's doggy day care."

"He also reminds me of Goldie," Charles said. "Like how she looks after a bath." Goldie was a golden retriever, the first puppy the Petersons had ever fostered. Now she lived next door, with Charles's best friend, Sammy.

Lizzie thought about that, then nodded. "You're right, I guess he does have that retriever nose and ears. I wonder if he's a golden doodle!"

"A *what*?" Dad asked from up front.

"It's a cross between a golden retriever and a poodle," Lizzie explained. "They're very popular lately. Some people also have Labradoodles."

"I can guess what *those* are a cross between," Mom said. "How do you *know* all this stuff, Lizzie?"

Lizzie just shrugged and smiled. She loved knowing all about dogs and dog breeds and dog training. She couldn't think of anything more interesting and fun.

Unless, she thought, looking down at the bundle on her lap, it was a new foster puppy!

CHAPTER FOUR

"Oh, my goodness," said Dr. Gibson, when she unwrapped the blankets. "Would you look at this little peanut? What a cutie-pie!"

Lizzie smiled at the vet. "I know," she said. "He's a sweetheart. He seems to trust us already."

"That's because you helped to rescue him," Dr. Gibson said.

Lizzie nodded. Maybe that was part of the reason she had fallen in love so fast. She knew she would never forget the way this pup had come into her life. What if she had never seen him swimming out there in the middle of the icy lake? Lizzie pushed the thought aside as she watched Dr. Gibson start her exam.

The vet sat the puppy on her examination table and put her stethoscope to his chest. She listened through the earpiece, cocking her head to one side. "His heart sounds good!" she said. She draped the stethoscope back around her neck and picked up another instrument. She looked into the puppy's ears and mouth, then shone a small flashlight into his eyes.

The puppy blinked.

Ooh, that's bright! But it's nice and warm in here, and this lady is gentle. Maybe soon my people will be here, and then we can all go home and have something to eat!

"I think he's going to be just fine," said Dr. Gibson, when she had finished her examination. "He's just all worn out from his adventures, and he's probably missed a meal or two. He'll get his energy back as soon as you feed him." She crossed her arms and leaned against the table. "But the question is, what was a puppy doing out there on the ice, all by himself? Where are his people?"

"That's what I've been wondering," Mom said. She was standing next to Lizzie, holding the Bean in her arms. The Bean's eyelids were drooping. He was ready for a snack and a nap. "I mean, this is just a tiny puppy! There must be someone out there who is very worried about him."

"He looks fairly well fed and groomed, so I don't think he's been on his own for very long," said Dr. Gibson. She frowned. "No collar, though. And I don't see a tattoo or any signs of a microchip."

"A microchip?" Dad asked.

"Some pet owners have a tiny electronic identification chip placed under their pet's skin," the vet explained. "It's only the size of a grain of rice, but it holds information about the pet and its owners. If a dog with a chip is ever lost, we can

use a monitor to read the chip and find out who the dog belongs to."

"Wow!" Dad looked impressed. "I never knew that."

"Microchipping has been around for a while," Lizzie told her dad. "We should think about it for Buddy. Or maybe we should just get him a tattoo."

"Like a fire-breathing dragon or something?" Charles asked. "Cool!"

Lizzie snorted. "It's not like a human tattoo. It's just a mark on his belly that identifies him as ours. You can use your phone number or address."

"Doesn't it hurt the dog?" Dad asked.

"Not really," said Dr. Gibson. "At least, they never act like it does when I use my little tattoo pen on them. I think it just feels sort of buzzy and tickly. Anyway, what about our little friend here? No chip, no tattoo, no collar. He doesn't look familiar to me at all, so I don't think he's

from around here." She gave the puppy a scratch between the ears. "He looks like one of those new mixes, maybe a golden doodle."

"That's exactly what *I* said!" Lizzie burst out.

"Well, you sure do know your dog breeds," Dr. Gibson told her. "These doodles often have some of the best qualities of both dogs in the mix. They're smart and goofy, like poodles, and very loyal and great with kids, like golden retrievers. And both breeds are athletic and love to play. If I were getting a new puppy, I might pick a doodle."

"Noodle!" the Bean said drowsily.

Everybody laughed. "No, it's *doodle*," Lizzie told her little brother.

"Noodle," the Bean insisted.

Lizzie thought for a second. She looked at the tired little puppy. "You know, that's not a bad name for this puppy! How about if we call him Noodle, since we don't know his real name right now?"

"I like it," said Dr. Gibson. "And now, I suggest you take this Noodle home and give him some puppy chow, some water, and a warm place to sleep. I predict that by tomorrow he'll be feeling one hundred percent himself, and his little dunking in the lake will be nothing but a memory."

On the way out of the vet's office, Lizzie stopped to look at the bulletin board. She always checked the signs there. People whose dogs were missing often put up a notice. But there was nothing there about Noodle. Maybe his people didn't even realize he was missing yet! Lizzie shuddered, imagining how upset she would be if Buddy disappeared someday.

"When we get home, maybe we should check with the police and Caring Paws," Dad suggested as they drove away. "Just in case someone has called looking for their dog." Caring Paws was the animal shelter where Lizzie volunteered every week. The people who worked there took care of lots of dogs and cats who needed homes. If somebody found a lost dog, they often brought it to the shelter. It would be safe there until its owners came to find it.

"Great idea," said Mom. "Maybe Lizzie can make some of her famous signs, too. Then we can put them up all around town and down at the lake."

Lizzie was known for making excellent signs on her computer. She was already picturing how this one might look, with a picture of Noodle and the words IS THIS YOUR PUPPY? across the top. As soon as she got home, she would use Dad's new digital camera to take some pictures.

She looked down at Noodle, who was nestled in her lap. He was dry and warm now, and his curly golden coat was soft and shiny, just the way Lizzie had pictured it. The poor puppy was absolutely exhausted from all the excitement. He had fallen asleep before Dad had even started the car!

"Don't you worry, little Noodle," Lizzie murmured as she stroked his silky ears. "We'll make sure you're safe and sound while we look for your people. That's a promise." Noodle opened his eyes and gazed at Lizzie. Then he sighed and settled in more comfortably on her lap.

What a scary day I had! But now I'm dry and warm, and too sleepy to feel scared anymore. Anyway, I feel safe with this girl. And I'm sure I'll be seeing my own people again soon.

CHAPTER FIVE

"Would you look at that guy *eat*?" Dad laughed and shook his head. The Petersons were all in the kitchen, watching Noodle gobble up the last bites from a dish of puppy food that Mom had put down just seconds ago. "Maybe we should have called him Hoover. He's like a vacuum cleaner!"

Lizzie giggled. It was true. She had never seen a puppy — or even a grown dog — eat so much, so fast. "He's a real chowhound, that's for sure. Or maybe he's just extra hungry from his adventures today."

"Sure, he must have worked up an appetite with all that swimming," said Mom.

Next to Noodle, Buddy was still picking away at his own bowl of puppy chow. Now that the

Petersons' puppy was a little more grown up, he was a very neat eater. "Remember when Buddy was little and he used to wade right into the food dish?" Charles asked. "Now look at him. He eats like a big boy."

The whole family turned to look fondly at Buddy. The Bean ran over to give him a hug. "Big boy!" he said. The sleeve of his Fur trailed into Buddy's dish.

"Don't bother Buddy while he's eating," Mom reminded the Bean, scooping him up and plopping him onto her lap. "Dogs don't like that."

"I think Noodle wants seconds," Lizzie said. Sure enough, the little curly-haired pup was sitting back on his bottom, gazing hopefully at Dad.

"Coming right up," Dad said, bending down to pick up Noodle's bowl. "I'll give him a little bit more. Dr. Gibson said not to feed him too much at once. If he hasn't eaten for a while, he could get sick if he eats too much too fast." He shook some

puppy chow into Noodle's dish and took it to the sink to add warm water. "There you go, pup," he said, putting it down.

It was gone in a flash. Noodle sat back and looked up hopefully. Would there be thirds?

Dad shook his head. "That's all for now, pal," he said. "How about some water?" He pushed Noodle's water bowl closer and Noodle stood up to lap at it for a few moments. Then the puppy sat back on his bottom again and looked around the room.

I'm still a little hungry, but I don't see any more food coming. I guess I can wait. And my people aren't here yet. Well, I guess I might as well check out this new place!

Noodle jumped up and zoomed out of the kitchen. "Hey!" Lizzie said, watching him zip past her. She laughed. "Look at him go. I guess he's feeling better."

“Wait for me!” the Bean yelled as he galloped after Noodle.

Buddy scrambled out from under the kitchen table, where he had been lying patiently under Charles’s feet ever since he’d finished his dinner. He let out a bark and dashed after the Bean.

Lizzie and Charles looked at each other, shrugged, and followed Buddy.

Noodle had run into the living room, and now he was investigating. He trotted from the couch to the rocking chair to the bookshelves to the fireplace, sniff-sniff-sniffing everything. When he sniffed under Mom’s blue easy chair, he started to sneeze so hard that he fell over — but he just rolled around for a second and then jumped to his feet, still sneezing.

What a silly puppy! The Bean clapped his hands and laughed his googly laugh. Lizzie and Charles were cracking up, too. Noodle ran around faster and sniffed harder and sneezed again and again. He seemed to enjoy the attention he was getting. This puppy was a real clown!

Ha-ha-ha! They like me. I love to make people laugh. Maybe if I do a somersault they'll laugh even harder! My people always liked that trick.

Suddenly, Noodle tripped on the rug and took a tumble, head over heels. For a second, Lizzie held her breath. Was the puppy okay? Then he jumped to his feet and shook his head so that his big floppy ears flipped and flapped. Lizzie started to laugh again. "You little silly!" she cried, running over to give Noodle a hug.

"He's funny," Charles said. "I wish we could keep him."

"Me, too!" said Lizzie.

"Lizzie, you not two," the Bean cried, holding up two fingers.

"I wasn't talking about how *old* I am," Lizzie said, scooping her little brother up into her arms,

along with Noodle. "You're a little silly, just like Noodle!"

The Bean giggled, then started squirming. "Let me go!"

Noodle started squirming, too. Lizzie kissed the top of the puppy's head. She kissed the Bean's ear, trying to hold her breath near his smelly Fur. Then she let them both go.

Noodle dashed off, with the Bean toddling after him. Then Buddy joined the parade. Noodle was like the Pied Piper — everybody wanted to follow him! Noodle ran around the couch three times, then over to the rocking chair, then did a loop around Mom's easy chair — almost knocking over her reading lamp — and galloped back toward the couch. At the last second, he scrunched down and slid right *under* the couch! Buddy dove right after him, but try as he might, the Bean could not squeeze in. He sat back on his butt and started to cry. His Fur was covered with dust balls.

Lizzie shook her head. "It's okay," she told

her little brother. “Don’t cry. The puppies will come out.”

Buddy popped out a few seconds later and jumped onto the Bean’s lap, licking the little boy’s face the way he always did when the Bean cried. Then Noodle popped out and danced around Buddy and the Bean, barking and wagging his tail.

“Well,” Dad said a few minutes later, as they watched Noodle start another game of Follow the Leader. “Dr. Gibson was right. He sure did get his energy back.”

Noodle kept the Petersons laughing all the way until bedtime. He was so much fun! Lizzie was so distracted that it wasn’t until she was almost asleep that night, cozy in her purple dog pajamas with her blankets pulled up to her chin, that she remembered. They had forgotten to call the police and Caring Paws! And now it was too late. Lizzie yawned and turned over. She would just have to remember to do it first thing in the morning.

CHAPTER SIX

Lizzie did remember, too. But it didn't do much good. When she called the Littleton police first thing on Sunday morning, the sergeant who answered told her that as far as he knew, nobody had called about a puppy. He said Sergeant Martin handled "missing pets and stuff like that," but he'd been out on vacation and would be back at work on Monday.

Next Lizzie called Caring Paws, the animal shelter. The director, Ms. Dobbins, said she hadn't gotten any calls, either — although she admitted that her desk was even more of a mess than usual and that there might be a note somewhere that she hadn't seen. She promised to look. And she told Lizzie that if the Petersons couldn't handle a foster puppy right then, she actually had room at the shelter for once and could take Noodle. "He sounds awfully cute," she said.

"Oh, we're happy to have him," Lizzie said quickly.

Noodle *was* awfully cute. When Lizzie finished her phone calls, she plopped right down on the kitchen floor and let Noodle climb all over her and lick her face and chew on her chin with his sharp little puppy teeth. "Ow! Ow! You little rascal!" Lizzie giggled. "Cut it out, now! You have to learn to be nice!"

I like to kiss and play and jump around. What's wrong with that? My people love *it when I chew them. Hey, what's that over there?*

Suddenly, Noodle jumped off Lizzie's lap and galumphed over to the far corner of the kitchen. He stuck his head under a cabinet and sniffed once, twice, three times. He sat back and barked.

Finally he stuck his head underneath the cabinet again and pulled with his whole body, growling little puppy growls as he dragged out an old toy of Buddy's — a duck that had once been fluffy and yellow but was now sort of dusty and matted.

"Well, look what you found! Who's a little smarty?" Dad had just come into the kitchen to start breakfast. "Looks like somebody deserves a blueberry pancake of his very own." Dad knew that dogs were not really supposed to eat people food, but he always made Buddy one little pancake on Sunday mornings, as a special treat.

"He *is* a smarty," Lizzie said. She felt proud of Noodle, as if he were her very own dog. Oh, if only he were!

Lizzie had not felt this way in a very long time. Usually, she understood perfectly that her family was only a foster family, and that the puppies they cared for did not belong to them and *would* not belong to them. But there was something about Noodle. Something really special.

How could it be that his people had not even called the police?

Maybe Noodle had been abandoned. Maybe his people did not love him or did not want him — although Lizzie couldn't imagine why *not.*

Maybe the way he had come into the Petersons' lives was proof that Noodle was *meant* to be part of their family.

Just then, Charles and the Bean came running into the kitchen, with Buddy on their heels. "Beat you!" the Bean cried happily.

"You sure did," Charles told his little brother. Then Charles winked at Lizzie, which meant, "only because I *let* him beat me."

Buddy ran right over to greet his new friend. He and Noodle bowed to each other, front legs splayed out in front and tails waving in the air behind. Then they took off running around the kitchen table, their toenails scrabbling on the floor as they dashed in circles. Lizzie loved seeing

Buddy play like that. He looked so happy! Maybe he was tired of being an "only dog." Maybe he needed a friend.

"Lizzie?" Dad was waving his hand in front of Lizzie's face. "Did you hear a word I just said to you?"

Oops. Lizzie shook her head.

Dad sighed. "Well, what I was saying was that we should probably find a collar for Noodle, so we can take him for walks on a leash. And then we really need to think about how we're going to find his family. They must be worried sick."

Charles spoke up. "Sammy said we could use one of Goldie's old collars," he said. "I already told him all about Noodle."

"Sounds good!" Dad said.

"Sammy also said that to solve the mystery we should go back to the scene of the crime," Charles said. "Like the police do. That's how you find clues."

"Scene of *what* crime?" Lizzie asked. She was confused. It wasn't like they had *stolen* Noodle — although she might have been tempted!

"I think what Sammy means is that we should go back to Loon Lake Park, where we found Noodle," Dad said. "You know, that's actually not a bad idea. Mom has a newspaper story to work on this morning, but I could take you down as soon as we finish breakfast. How about it?"

Sammy came over just in time to help polish off the last of the pancakes. On weekends, Sammy almost always had two breakfasts: one at home and one at the Petersons'. Then Charles read the funnies to Buddy and Noodle; that was *his* Sunday tradition. Finally, they all piled into the van and headed for Loon Lake Park.

Soon Lizzie was standing on the shore of the icy lake again, remembering how scared she'd been when she first saw Noodle swimming out in that open patch of water. "But you made it," she said to the puppy, who was standing next to her on the other end of the leash. She held on tightly. Noodle wasn't going *anywhere* without her, Lizzie thought. She already loved him too much to even *think* of him in danger again.

Now Noodle tugged on the leash.

Come on! I know this place. I'll show you around.

Lizzie followed the pup as he pulled her along the shoreline. Before long she had traveled much farther than she and Buddy had gone the day before.

"Lizzie! Where are you going?" Charles yelled from the dock, near where he and Sammy were playing fetch with Buddy.

"Ask Noodle!" Lizzie yelled back. "He seems to know!"

Noodle pulled Lizzie past the picnic areas, past the campground, even past the row of tall pines shading a point of land jutting into the lake.

He pulled her through prickly sticker bushes, through patches of dirty snow, over hummocks of tall, rustly dried grass, and around the big gray boulders that lined the shore.

Suddenly Lizzie realized that they'd come almost all the way around the lake. They were in sight of the cabin with the moose antlers! She had never even *been* that far from the park area. "Noodle!" she said. "Would you mind telling me —"

But Noodle wasn't pulling anymore. He sat back on his butt and started barking.

Look! Look! That's mine! See why I brought you here?

"Noodle!" Lizzie said, panting a little. "What is going on?" Then she followed his gaze and saw what he was barking at. Just ahead a fallen tree lay on its side, with its roots and trunk on the shore and its bare branches hanging just over

the icy lake. Tangled in one branch — the one farthest out over the ice — was a faded purple collar.

"What's that?" Lizzie stared at the collar. Noodle danced around, barking loudly. "Are you telling me that's your collar?" Noodle barked some more.

Lizzie looked out at the collar. It would only take a few steps to get to it, but there was no way Lizzie was going to risk walking on the frozen lake. She was not interested in falling in like Noodle had. But she had to get that collar! Lizzie tied Noodle's leash to a nearby tree so he couldn't run off. Then she scrambled up onto the fallen tree trunk and began to inch her way out over the ice.

The tree trunk got smaller and smaller as Lizzie moved along. Lizzie had always been good at climbing trees, but she had never climbed a *side-ways* tree before!

Suddenly, the tree shifted beneath her weight.

"Whoa!" Lizzie grabbed on to the tree and froze

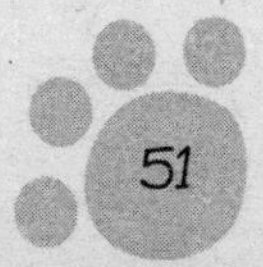

in place. She looked down at the icy surface below. It looked solid, but what would happen if she tumbled onto it? She pictured the cold, black water that had nearly swallowed Noodle the day before. Suddenly, she felt too scared to move.

CHAPTER SEVEN

Lizzie did not like being stuck out there, hanging over the ice on that tree trunk. She took a deep breath and inched backward until she felt safe again. Phew! That was better. But her job was not done. She looked out at the collar. Even if she stretched, she would not be able to reach out and touch it.

Lizzie glanced back across the lake, to where her dad and the boys were waiting. Should she go get help? No! She could do it herself.

Lizzie thought for a second. Then, holding on to the tree with one hand, she reached out and broke off one of its long, dead branches. Perfect!

She stretched out again along the tree trunk and pointed the stick at the collar. The tip of the branch just barely brushed the tags hanging from the collar, and they jingled — but the collar stayed put.

Back on shore, Noodle would not stop barking and dancing around. He *really* wanted her to get that collar.

Lizzie tried again, poking the stick carefully beneath the collar and jiggling it free from the tangle of branches. On her third try, she hooked the collar! Now all she had to do was pull it back toward her — without dropping it down onto the ice.

Lizzie concentrated. Carefully, she guided the collar closer, until she could grab it. Then she dropped the stick and inched backward, clutching her prize.

Finally, Lizzie was back on solid ground, next to Noodle. She had tree bark in her hair, her hands were scratched, and there was a new tear on the front of her jacket that Mom would *not* be happy about.

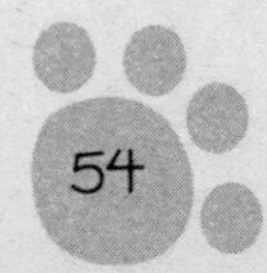

But she had the collar.

Noodle came sniffing over.

Mine! Mine! I knew it! Oh, this smells like my people! Maybe we're getting closer to them!

The puppy's tail wagged double-time as he nuzzled the collar. "Well, I guess it must be yours," Lizzie said. "Why else would you act like this?" She turned the collar over in her hands. There were blond, curly hairs stuck in the nylon material — Noodle's hairs! They matched his coat exactly. The collar was definitely his.

So, in one second, when she read the tags, Lizzie would know who Noodle's owners were. That was good, right? Then why did Lizzie feel like there was a rock in her stomach?

She reached out to scratch Noodle's head. She kissed the soft fur just behind his ear. "Maybe I'm just not quite ready to give you up," she whispered. Noodle licked Lizzie's cheek, and when she smelled his sweet puppy breath she felt as if her heart might burst.

Lizzie had never thought she could love any puppy as much as she loved Buddy. But Noodle was a very special dog. She didn't love Buddy any less — but there was definitely room in her heart for this puppy she had helped to rescue.

Noodle nudged Lizzie's hand, and the tags on the collar jingled. Lizzie took a deep breath. Yes, Noodle was special. But that probably meant that his owners loved him very much, too. And it would be wrong to wait any longer to let them know he was safe.

Lizzie turned over one of the tags. It was the kind that proves that a dog has had all the shots it needs. "Rabies vaccination," she read. "Expires — hey!" She looked closely at the date. "That's, like, two *years* ago!" She looked at Noodle. She wasn't sure of his exact age, but he was definitely not two years old. Quickly, she turned over the other tag. The writing on it was almost worn

off, but she could just make out some letters. "B-L . . . K-I-E," she read. "Blackie?" And there was a phone number, or at least part of one.

"Blackie!" Lizzie said. "But — why would anyone call *you* Blackie?" She stared at Noodle, then back at the collar in her hand. The gold hairs trapped in the cloth glinted in the sun.

"Ohhh," Lizzie said. "I get it." Suddenly, she figured it out. This *was* the collar Noodle had been wearing. But it had once belonged to some other dog. Obviously, Noodle's people *didn't* love him. They didn't even care enough about him to get him his own collar, with his own tags. They must have thought that a faded old hand-me-down was good enough.

Lizzie was disgusted. She gathered Noodle onto her lap and gave him a big hug. "You deserve better than that," she whispered into his ear. "You deserve the best collar in the world, with shiny new tags that say *your* name." Noodle licked Lizzie's cheek and nibbled on her chin. Lizzie laughed. "Okay, I get it. You don't really care, do you? But I do. I care a lot."

She got to her feet and Noodle jumped up, too, eager to go wherever Lizzie was going. Together, they walked all the way back around the shore of Loon Lake, back to where the others were waiting.

"Look what Noodle found!" Lizzie said. Dad and Charles and Sammy were perched on a picnic table, throwing sticks for Buddy.

Lizzie climbed onto the table and handed the collar to Dad, telling him all about where she'd found it.

"I'm not sure your Mom would be thrilled to hear about you climbing sideways trees over the ice," he said. But Lizzie could tell he was kind of proud of her.

Then Dad took a closer look at the collar, with Charles and Sammy leaning over his shoulder. "Interesting," he said. "It sure looks like Noodle

was wearing this, even though I can't imagine anyone calling him Blackie. Plus, it looks way too big for Noodle."

"Exactly," Lizzie said. "That's probably why it slipped off. It's a hand-me-down collar."

"So now we can just call the number on the tag and find Noodle's owners!" Charles ruffled Noodle's ears. "That's good news."

Lizzie did not exactly agree, but she kept that to herself. How many times had she told Charles that he "just had to understand" that they weren't going to be allowed to keep the foster puppies they cared for? Now here she was, wishing more than anything that she could keep Noodle forever.

"That may be easier said than done," Dad said, peering at the tag with the phone number on it. "This number is kind of worn off."

When they got home, Dad took the name tag off the collar. Mom joined them at the kitchen table

while they passed it around, looking at it under a magnifying glass. The Bean squirmed his way onto Lizzie's lap so he could see.

"Ugh! Mom, the Bean is really starting to stink!" Lizzie said. "Can't we *please* wash his Fur?" She didn't even want to *touch* it. Was that toothpaste all down the front? And a piece of gum stuck to one sleeve? Gross.

"No!" the Bean said firmly.

Mom shrugged. "I did tell him it was his choice," she reminded Lizzie. "I have to stick to that. It's only fair. May I remind you that you ran around in pink cowboy boots and a tutu for pretty much the whole time you were three? Why? Because I agreed that you could. A deal's a deal in my book."

"Deal!" Bean agreed, nodding hard. His lower lip was stuck out far enough to trip on. Any minute now, he might start wailing.

Lizzie sighed. "All right! Sorry! Forget I said anything! It's okay, sweetie, don't worry." She

patted the Bean's back, trying to avoid the crustiest spots on his Fur.

Dad was still looking at the dog tag. "So, I can read the last part of this phone number all right," he reported. "I think it's five-five-five, seven-two-two-seven. But the area code is just about totally gone. I think it starts with eight, though."

"So — how many area codes can there be, starting with eight?" Charles said. "No big deal. We'll just try them all."

CHAPTER EIGHT

Charles's plan made sense to Lizzie. And she knew that trying to find Noodle's owners was the right thing to do. So right after lunch, she sat down and started dialing. She was using the kitchen phone, because Dad's cell phone — which the whole family usually used for long-distance calls — had completely run out of power, and Dad *still* couldn't find his charger.

"Hello?"

Lizzie swallowed hard, suddenly realizing that she should have thought about what she was going to say *before* she dialed the first number on her list. She had started with area code 802, Vermont. She could have tried 801, but that was

Utah, and that seemed *way* too far away for Noodle's owners to live.

"Um, hello," she said. "I was just wondering, do you have a dog named Blackie? Or, I mean, did you *used* to have a dog named Blackie, and now you have a puppy? Like, um, maybe a golden doodle? But he's missing?"

"Excuse me? Is this some kind of prank call?" The woman on the other end of the line sounded completely confused, and Lizzie couldn't blame her. But obviously this was not Noodle's owner. Otherwise the name Blackie and the mention of a missing puppy would have meant something to her.

"Never mind," Lizzie said quickly. "Wrong number, I guess." She hung up and looked at the list of numbers on the pad by the phone. Then she crossed off the first area code: 802. There were at least fifteen more to try.

Lizzie sighed. To be honest she didn't really

even *want* to find Noodle's real owners. She glanced over at the dog bed in the corner of the kitchen, where Noodle was snoozing after his own lunch. His puppy belly was full and round, and his big soft paws were twitching. Lizzie knew that meant he was probably dreaming about running.

"Chasing squirrels, Noodle?" she said softly. She could have watched him all day, even when he was just lying there sleeping! He was such a sweet puppy.

Noodle's nose twitched, and he opened one eye to look back at her. Lizzie laughed. That made Noodle jump right up and gallop over to say hello.

Hi! Hi! Hi! How about some pats? I love the way you pat me. It reminds me of the way my people pat me. Think I'll see them again soon? I sure hope so. I mean, I like you a lot, but as nice as you are, you're not my people!

Lizzie reached down and pulled the little pup onto her lap. "You are the *cutest*!" she said. "I mean, next to Buddy, that is." She kissed the top of his head. "And you smell so good! Especially compared to the Bean." They really had to do something about that Fur.

Meanwhile, it was time to try another phone call. This time, Lizzie tried to figure out what she would say *before* she dialed. But the second call did not go much better than the first.

"Hello?" The man who answered spoke loudly and sounded annoyed.

"Hello, my name is Lizzie Peterson, and I found a puppy — or rather a purple collar — well, both, really, and —"

Click. The man hung up before Lizzie could even finish.

"How's it going, Miss Lizzie?" Dad came into the kitchen, wiping his hands on a rag. He had been working on his pickup truck out in the driveway.

Lizzie sighed. "Not very well, I guess."

"Tell you what," Dad said. "Why don't I try for a bit? Maybe folks would listen a little better to a grown-up. Anyway, we need some of your famous signs. How about if you head upstairs and get to work on the computer, and I'll take over on the phone?"

Lizzie was happy to hand over her list of area codes. "Come on, Noodle," she said. "Let's go upstairs."

Noodle scrambled to his feet and followed Lizzie out of the kitchen.

Sure, sure, I'll go anywhere with you! What are we doing next? Maybe we're going to see my people!

Upstairs, Lizzie got out the camera and posed Noodle on the blue rag rug next to her bed. "First we need a great picture," she said. "Look at me, Noodle!"

Noodle jumped up and ran over to Lizzie, sticking his nose right up into the camera.

Lizzie giggled. "No, Noodle! You have to sit!" She put him back into position. Then she stepped away and looked through the camera again, focusing on Noodle's adorable face. "Ready?" she asked.

Noodle jumped up again. This time Lizzie just put down the camera and gave him a big hug. "You are the silliest!" she said. She lay down on the floor and let Noodle dance around her, snuffling at her hair and licking her ears. It was so much more fun to play with Noodle than to make a dumb sign looking for his owners — who probably didn't even care about him, anyway!

"Noodle?"

Lizzie looked up to see the Bean peering around the corner of her door. "Come on in," she said. "Want to play with Noodle?"

"Yeah!" The Bean ran into the room. "Noodle!" He threw his arms around the puppy.

Noodle squirmed away.

Pee-yoo! Sometimes I like yucky smells, but a delicious pile of garbage is one thing, and a stinky human is another. This little boy does not smell very good. Not like my *people.*

"Uppy?" the Bean asked. He tried again, reaching forward to give Noodle a big hug. But Noodle stepped away, and the Bean plopped down on his behind, looking sad and bewildered. "Uppy no play?"

Lizzie had a feeling she knew *exactly* why the uppy didn't want to be near the Bean. "I think it's your Fur," she told her little brother gently. "I think Noodle doesn't like the way it smells."

"But — but — but —" The Bean looked as if he might start screaming any minute.

"I'm not telling you to wash it." Lizzie held up her hands. "That's your choice. But you know, every puppy needs a bath *once* in a while!"

CHAPTER NINE

The next day was Monday, and Lizzie and Charles had to go to school. Lizzie could hardly *stand* to miss one minute with Noodle. Before she left, she kissed and hugged him so much that Buddy got jealous and came over to put his paws up on her knee. He wanted attention, too.

"Of course I'll kiss you, too, Buddy," Lizzie said, kneeling down. "I'll always love you best of all. But" — she bent down to whisper into his soft brown ear — "wouldn't you love to have a little brother?"

All day in school, Lizzie daydreamed about what it would be like if Noodle could live with the Petersons forever. When her parents first agreed that Buddy could stay, it had been like a dream

come true. Having a dog of their own was the best thing that had ever happened to Charles and Lizzie and the Bean. So — what about having *two* dogs? Lizzie could hardly even imagine how much fun *that* would be.

So far, none of the phone calls they had made had turned up Noodle's people. Maybe the Petersons would never find out who they were! Or, better yet, Lizzie pictured this: They *would* find them, but the people would say they just really couldn't take care of a dog. They would ask if the Petersons knew anyone who wanted to adopt Noodle. "Well," Mom would say, "I never thought we could handle one dog, much less two, but — we'd *love* to have Noodle!"

By the time school ended, Lizzie had practically convinced herself that Noodle was already hers — or at least that he would soon be hers forever. But she had figured out that it would probably be best if she *did* find his people, just so she would know for *sure* that he really needed a home. She had a plan, too! During math period, when she should have been practicing fractions, she had been thinking dreamily about the day before at the lake, when she had found Noodle's collar.

Suddenly, she had remembered that she had seen paw prints in the snow near the tree. There was still enough snow on the ground that maybe, just maybe, she could find *more* paw prints — and follow them to find out where Noodle had come from!

On the way home after school, Lizzie admitted to Charles that she was hoping they could keep Noodle forever.

"But even if you find Noodle's owners and they don't want him, do you really think Mom would let us have another dog?" Charles asked as he and Lizzie arrived at their front door.

"I bet I could talk her into it," Lizzie said as she pushed the door open. "Hi, we're home!" she yelled. "Buddy! Noodle!"

The two puppies came galloping into the front

hall, with the Bean running after them. Both puppies were barking, and the Bean was squealing with laughter. Noodle ran right up to Lizzie and Charles.

Yay! You're home! Time to play! If only my people were here to play with us, too, then this place would be perfect!

Charles let Noodle lick his cheek. Then he made a funny face. "Um, what's that yucky smell?" he asked, wrinkling his nose.

Lizzie didn't say a word. She just pointed to the Bean and his matted Fur.

"Oh," said Charles. "Right." He leaned away from his little brother. Buddy and Noodle were edging away from the Bean, too.

The Bean frowned. Lizzie saw him sniff the arm of his Fur. Maybe, just maybe, he was almost ready to give in and let the stinky sweater be washed.

Lizzie's mom came out of the kitchen. "Lizzie, I called the police station again," she said.

Lizzie felt her insides go all mushy. "You did?" she asked. "Did they hear anything about any missing puppies?"

Mom shook her head. "Sergeant Martin was supposed to be back today, but he called in sick. The officer who answered said he didn't think anyone had called about a missing dog over the weekend."

Lizzie let out a breath. What a relief! If the police had gotten a call about Noodle, that would mean his people were looking for him, and that they *did* care about him, and that they probably would want to take their puppy back instead of letting the Petersons adopt him.

Lizzie pulled Noodle onto her lap and gave him a great big hug.

"I know, it's disappointing," said Mom. "We all want to find Noodle's people as quickly as possible. Think how much he must miss them!"

Lizzie tried not to. Instead, she sent Noodle a thought message: *Think about this: how much I love you!*

Noodle squirmed deeper into Lizzie's arms.

Mmmm, nice hugs. My people used to hug me like that. Even though this girl is nice, I still miss them!

"Mom, can you drive me and Charles to Loon Lake Park? There's something I want to check out down there." Lizzie put Noodle down and stood up. "And we can take the dogs for a walk, too."

"By yourselves?" Mom looked doubtful. "Will you promise to be careful around that ice?"

"Of course!" said Lizzie. "I won't go near it. Do you think I want to fall in?"

"Well, okay," Mom said. "I have some grocery shopping to do. I'll drop you off."

On the way to the lake, Lizzie and Charles rode

in the way back of Mom's van, near the dog crate that held Buddy and Noodle. It was as if they were *all* trying to stay as far away as possible from the stinky Bean in his car seat.

"See you in half an hour!" Mom said as she let them off at the lake. "Be careful!" she called as she drove away with the Bean.

"That should be just enough time," Lizzie said. She was holding Noodle's leash, and Charles was holding Buddy's. "Let's go!"

Once again, Noodle pulled on his leash, dragging Lizzie along the shoreline. She noticed that the ice was beginning to melt at the edges of the lake. It was hard to believe that in a few short months she would be swimming in the cool, clear water! Most of the snow on the shore had melted away, too. Lizzie was disappointed. That meant they probably wouldn't find any tracks.

"Where are we *going*?" Charles asked, stumbling along behind Lizzie.

A few minutes later, they arrived at the fallen

tree. "See, this is where the collar was." Lizzie pointed to the branches hanging over the ice.

"All the way out there? How did you *get* it?" Charles asked.

"It wasn't easy." Lizzie remembered inching her way out on that tree trunk. Then she remembered something else: the way the tags had jingled when she poked at the collar with a stick. One tag would not make a jingling sound. There had been *two*! She had forgotten all about the other tag.

"Charles! That collar! Besides that name tag, there was *another* tag on it. A rabies vaccination tag."

Charles's eyes lit up. "Really? Maybe it'll give us another clue about who Noodle belongs to! Where is it?"

"It's back home," Lizzie said. "Remember? Dad hung the collar on a nail in the garage, since it was too big for Noodle anyway."

Suddenly, Lizzie didn't mind anymore about not finding any tracks. She couldn't wait to get

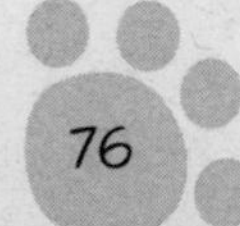

home to take a look at the other tag on that purple collar.

Dad was home by the time Lizzie and Charles got back from the lake. Lizzie ran straight for the garage and grabbed the collar. "See?" she said, when she was back in the kitchen. She showed it to her dad. "We forgot about the other tag!" Her words tumbled out as she explained. She picked up the magnifying glass on the table and looked at the tag. "Boston!" she said. "This says the dog was registered in Boston. Maybe Noodle's owners are summer people who were up at one of the cabins for the weekend!"

Dad peered at the tag. "Huh. You may be right." He grabbed the phone book and flipped some pages. "Ok, here's a Boston area code that starts with eight. Let's try that number!" He went right to the phone and dialed.

Inside her jacket pocket, Lizzie crossed her fingers. Was this it? The moment of truth when they would find Noodle's owners?

But Dad shook his head. "No answer." He was still holding the phone to his ear. Then he held up a finger. "Hold on, there's a machine!" He waited for a second, then said, "Hello, my name is Paul Peterson from Littleton, near Loon Lake. Have you lost a puppy? We've found him, and he's safe and sound. Call us!" Quickly, he rattled off his phone number and hung up.

"Now what?" Lizzie asked.

Dad just shrugged. "I guess we just have to wait to see if we hear back," he said.

CHAPTER TEN

"Anything?" Lizzie asked as soon as she got home from school the next day. "Did anybody call?"

"Not yet," said her mother.

Lizzie could hardly stand it. She had thought they were so close to finding Noodle's owners, but why hadn't anybody called back? Lizzie sat at the kitchen table, fiddling nervously with the purple collar. Finally, she couldn't stand sitting still for one more minute. She had to *do* something. "Buddy!" she called. "Noodle!" Both puppies came galloping into the kitchen. "Look at you two," Lizzie said. "Your paws are all muddy from being at the lake yesterday. How about a bath?"

"Now *that* sounds like a good idea," said her

mother. “Maybe Charles can help. Just be careful and —”

“Keep the door closed!” Lizzie laughed. She knew Mom was remembering the last time Lizzie had given two puppies a bath. They had managed to escape and run through the house, splattering soapy water everywhere.

Charles ran the water while Lizzie gathered towels and puppy shampoo. Then she rounded up Buddy and Noodle and brought them into the steamy bathroom. She and Charles had just lifted Noodle into the tub and then Buddy, when there was a knock at the door.

“Bath time?” the Bean asked, when Lizzie opened the door a crack. “Bath time for puppies?”

Lizzie's eyes widened. Why not? There was more than one way to wash a Fur!

“Yes!” she said. “That's right! Bath time for puppies!” And a few minutes later, the Bean joined Buddy and Noodle in the tub — with his

Fur on! The two puppies and the little boy wriggled in the suds while Lizzie rubbed puppy shampoo into the Bean's Fur and started to scrub. Good-bye, oatmeal! Good-bye, grape juice! Good-bye, milk and toothpaste and dog food!

Puppy bath time was noisy and wet and took quite a long time. Finally, while Charles and Lizzie were rubbing the puppies and the Bean with towels, Mom called from downstairs. "Lizzie! Charles! Can you come right down? We have company!"

Noodle, still a little damp, led the way downstairs. Lizzie saw a round, dark-haired woman waiting in the front hall. There was a girl next to her, about Lizzie's age, with the same dark hair.

"Lizzie, this is Mrs. Rispoli," Mom said. "She just drove all the way up from Boston. And this is her daughter, Sophia."

Lizzie's heart thumped. Instantly, she knew exactly who these Rispoli people must be. They were Noodle's owners. The people who didn't care about him. The people who had totally abandoned him.

But Mrs. Rispoli was rushing toward Noodle. "Oh, there he is!" She scooped him up before he even got to the bottom of the stairs. "You darling!" She kissed him over and over on the top of his head. Sophia squeezed in so she could kiss Noodle, too. "I don't believe it!" cried Mrs. Rispoli. "This is so amazing! I hope it's okay that we drove straight here. I tried to call, but I kept getting voice mail. So we just drove up to Littleton and asked where the Petersons live — and here we are!" She kissed Noodle all over and hugged him tight.

Lizzie could see tears rolling down Mrs. Rispoli's face. There was no question about it: This woman was glad to see her puppy. Lizzie suddenly realized that Dad must have left his *cell phone* number when he left that message. And Dad's cell phone was dead and he *still* couldn't find his charger. That explained why they hadn't heard from anyone.

Noodle was kissing Mrs. Rispoli and Sophia back, covering their faces with huge, slurpy licks. His tail was wagging a mile a minute.

Oh, joy! Oh, joy! My people are here! Oh, joy!

"Boy, Noodle sure is happy to see you!" Lizzie couldn't help feeling a tiny bit jealous.

"Noodle?" Sophia looked confused.

Lizzie blushed. "Oh — that's what we were calling him," she explained.

"What a *great* name!" Mrs. Rispoli held Noodle up in the air and rubbed noses with him. "We called him Bronson, but it never really seemed to fit. Maybe he really is a Noodle, after all." She hugged him close again. "No matter what his name is, we are just so, so happy to see him again! I thought he was gone forever."

"But if he ran away, why . . ." Lizzie realized it might be rude to ask why the Rispolis had not looked for their puppy.

"Why didn't I look for him?" Mrs. Rispoli asked. "I did! I looked and looked!" She put Noodle down and watched with tears in her eyes as he ran off to wrestle with Buddy.

"I drove up to our house on Loon Lake last Friday morning, just to pick up some extra chairs we needed for a huge surprise party for my mother's birthday," Mrs. Rispoli explained. "We'd been planning the party for months. Bronson — I mean, Noodle — came with me. When we left Boston, I couldn't find his collar, so I just put our old dog Blackie's collar on him.

"Up at the lake house, I was loading chairs into my car when that naughty puppy ran off. I tried to follow his tracks, but he was nowhere to be seen."

Lizzie had her hand over her mouth. What a

story! She would have been *heartbroken* if she ever lost Buddy like that.

"I called and I called, and I looked all over, but there was no sign of him. I phoned the police and left a description, but they hadn't heard anything. I even stayed overnight, even though I hadn't planned to, and looked some more on Saturday morning. My throat was raw and sore from calling for him. But by noon, I couldn't stay any longer. I had to leave things in the hands of the police and hope for the best so I could get home in time for the party, even though nobody was going to feel much like celebrating." Mrs. Rispoli blew her nose into the wad of tissues she was clutching. "Oh, how I hated to tell Sophia and her father."

Lizzie finished the story. "I guess your information just got lost at the police station, because of the weekend and Sergeant Martin being out and everything. But luckily we found Noodle later on

Saturday afternoon, swimming around in a spot of open water, over by the park. He must have spent Friday night outside, wandering around and trying to find his way home."

Mrs. Rispoli started crying again. "I know! Your mother just told us all about the rescue! Isn't it amazing? And he's perfectly fine!" She shook her head, smiling through her tears. "It's wonderful."

"So —" Lizzie almost hated to ask, mainly because she thought she already knew the answer. "I guess you want to keep him?"

Mrs. Rispoli stared at Lizzie. "Keep him? Of course! We'll never let him out of our sight again!" Then her eyes softened. "Oh, I see," she said. "Did you think he had been abandoned?"

Lizzie nodded, turning her face away to hide the tears that seemed to be leaking out of her eyes. She couldn't talk. She reached out to pick Noodle up one last time. She knew she had been silly to even *think* about Noodle being hers

forever. That was not how this foster puppy thing worked. It was all about finding the best home for each dog. And Noodle *had* a wonderful home. Lizzie knew that now. She could tell by the way Mrs. Rispoli and Sophia looked at him that Noodle would always be loved and cared for. She couldn't hold on to him the way the Bean had held on to his Fur. She had to give this puppy up.

Lizzie buried her nose in Noodle's soft, sweet-smelling neck, giving him one last kiss. Tears welled up in her eyes. She tried to hold them back, but one of them dropped onto Noodle's nose.

"Tell you what, Lizzie," Mrs. Rispoli said, kneeling down so that she was looking straight at Lizzie. "We'll be at our cabin all summer. It's the little one with the moose antlers. Do you know the one I mean?"

Lizzie wiped away another tear and nodded. "I love that cabin."

"Well, I hope you and your brothers and

Buddy will be regular visitors. Don't you agree, Sophia?"

Sophia nodded eagerly. "We can teach Buddy and Noodle to jump off our dock, the way Blackie used to." She smiled shyly at Lizzie.

Mrs. Rispoli reached over and gave Noodle a pat. "And I know for sure that Bronson — I mean, Noodle — will always be happy to see you and his new best puppy friend, Buddy."

Wow! Lizzie couldn't believe her luck. Finally she would find out what it was like to be at one of those cool Loon Lake cabins — with Buddy! Plus, she would still be able to watch Noodle grow up. She started to feel a little bit better.

Lizzie sniffed and nodded. "That sounds good," she said. She tried to smile. "Thank you." It was time. She gave Noodle one last hug, then walked over to put him gently into Sophia's arms.

"No," said Mrs. Rispoli, leaning down to kiss the top of Noodle's head. "Thank *you,* for saving our precious puppy."

PUPPY TIPS

If your dog runs off or gets lost:

• Call the police and tell them about your missing pet. Give as much information as you can: his name, what he looks like, where he was last seen, and his personality (a shy dog might only come to a stranger who is holding a treat, while a friendly dog is easier to approach).

• Call your local Humane Society or animal shelter to find out if your dog was found and brought there.

• Make some signs that list all the same information you told the police, along with a photograph. Put them up in your neighborhood, in the place where you last saw your dog, and in any other areas that are familiar to her (like a park where you take her to play with other dogs). Make sure to put your phone number on the sign! It can be helpful to offer even a small reward.

If you find a missing dog:

- Approach the dog carefully, as you would with any dog you don't know. Make sure it is friendly. Ask an adult for help.

- If the dog is wearing a collar, check the dog's tags. Some dogs wear tags with their owner's name and phone number.

- Call the police and your local Humane Society and let them know you have found a missing dog. If you can't keep the dog in your house or yard, take it to the shelter.

- Put up some signs about the dog you found.

Dear Reader,

When Django, my black Lab, was only about six months old, he fell through the ice just like Noodle did! It was in a much smaller pond than Loon Lake. For a moment, I thought I was going to have to jump in after him, but fortunately he was able to scrabble his way back onto shore.

I thought Django might be scared of water after that, but he wasn't. Most black Labs love to swim! Do you know a dog that likes to swim?

Yours from the Puppy Place,
Ellen Miles

ABOUT THE AUTHOR

Ellen Miles lives in Vermont. She is the author of more than twenty books including the Taylor-Made Tales series, *The Pied Piper*, and other Scholastic Classics.

Ellen has always loved a good story. She also loves biking, skiing, and playing with her own dog, Django. Django is a black Lab who would rather eat a book than read one.